The
Resurrectionist

Also by Kathy L. Brown

Water of Life: A Novelette (Sean Joye
Investigations Series, Book Two)

The Resurrectionist

Kathy L. Brown

Otter Springs Publishing
St. Louis

To my father. Thanks for all the stories.

Acknowledgements

One of my father's many jobs in life was as a prison guard at the Southern Illinois Penitentiary in Chester, Illinois. *The Resurrectionist* grew from a tiny seed of a story about those days, which he planted in my mind when I was a child.

Missouri State Penitentiary Tours' (https://www.missouripentours.com/history-tours/) staff members were invaluable to the research for this story. As this book goes to press, the facility is recovering from tornado damage suffered in May of 2019. A portion of this book's profits will be donated to the restoration work or similar projects.

Thanks to my sensitivity reader, Kayla, from Orphans and Widows Media. (Visit her at https://tinyurl.com/sensitivityread.) Kayla, as well as Dan Brown, Patrick Brown, Carol Kruchowski, Deb Schuey, Lisa Parker Scott, Brian Stamper, Kathy Van Voorhees, and LZ, tried to keep me on the straight and narrow; any errors in fact, syntax, or sentiment are my own.

Turn here," the Judge said from the back seat as he tapped me on the shoulder. "You're about to miss the prison entrance." Obedient ever, I veered left, the Model T skidding across the melting asphalt only to lurch over the gravel road's ruts. At the sight of a chain gang marching toward us, I slammed the brake, and the tires spewed a cloud of dust into the air. The walking boss—on horseback today, no fool in the summer heat—tipped his hat and hurried them along.

Four denim-clad white men stumbled over the gravel and their chains but managed to hang onto the rectangular pine box they carried. Another inmate, a tall, freckled ginger laden with shovels and pickaxes, hurried behind them.

"You'd think they'd assign trusties to the burial detail," the Judge said. "Then they wouldn't have to chain them together."

At the time, I'd only been in the States a few months. All I knew about the American penal system was the getting nicked part, but I'd heard somewhere that convicts could gain special status and privileges, even authority over other inmates, through the trusty system. Whether the grift operated on good behavior, bribes, or extraordinary kowtowing, I couldn't say. "Maybe they don't trust all that many prisoners."

I continued to watch the men as they made for a small burial plot atop a rise about fifty feet off the road. The ugliest tree I'd ever seen in my life—half-dead, misshapen, and sprouting wicked thorns at odd intervals—crowned the hilltop but provided not a whit of shade from the noonday sun. Crumbling limestone grave markers poked out of its base. I pictured the roots, slow but sure, crushing the flimsy pine boxes and the poor sods under the hillside.

Just thinking on the fella they were about to plant among strangers in this godforsaken place gave me the heebie-jeebies. A wisp of a cloud must have passed over the sun; shadows covered the graveyard for a moment. But what should have been a small blessing felt like a threat.

"Anytime now, Sean," the Judge said. The walking boss and his horse had trotted across the road while I'd been worrying over a dead tree and a dead man.

"Sorry." I stepped on the gear shift and gave the car some petrol. "Thought that cloud might bring us some rain."

"Rain's unlikely," the Judge said. I drove another hundred yards or so and then stopped at the prison gate. My palms, damp with sweat, stuck to the steering wheel. Of course, I'm sweating, I told myself. The day's hot as hell. Got nothing to do with my pounding heart or a dead man crossing my path.

While I waited for a guard to decide to open the gates, I watched the burial detail in the rearview window. The men had set down their burden, and three of them commenced to digging. The boss got off his horse and motioned the other two cons over to the pine box. They dragged themselves and their chains to the boss, giving the coffin a wide berth. There was a bit of conversation, and the ginger seemed to offer to take over the digging. The boss knocked him up the side of the head and again pointed at the box. The inmate slowly walked over to it and even more slowly lifted the lid for the boss to peek in.

I about jumped out of my skin at a tapping noise on the windscreen. "How's y'all doing today?" said the gate guard as he motioned me out of the car. He wore a name badge that said "Gillespie" and a sweat-stained khaki uniform. "Come for the hanging?"

I nodded. "This here's the Judge. From St. Louis."

"Well, youse right welcome here." Gillespie consulted a list, peered in at the Judge, and nodded. "I'll just check you for weapons," he said to me, "and y'all can be on your way."

I leaned, arms outstretched, across the car's hood. On the Judge's order, I hadn't even brought a gun—it wouldn't be allowed inside the prison. Driving all the way from St. Louis to Jefferson City without a weapon was foolish, and the risk had set me on edge for half the day already. That's what I told myself, anyway.

The guard chuckled in my ear. "I might think you done this before."

Quite true and none of his business. I watched the Judge through the windscreen, comfortable and out of the sun in the car's back seat. He avoided my eyes.

Gillespie searched me right quick, all the while yammering about the hanging. "This should be a good'un. Yes, sir, the whole state of Missourah will sleep better once that—that—sumbitch nun-killer swings."

The Judge gazed at the rows of prison factory buildings in the near distance where the unpaid labor churned out everything from shoes to buggy whips.

"Well, this is the judge what sentenced him," I told the guard as I opened the car door.

"Did he now?" Gillespie took another look at His Honor, Judge James Dolan of the Twenty-Second Circuit Court. "He done us a public service then, sure enough."

The quality of the frisk was second-rate at best, and I slid back behind the steering wheel with a folding knife in my coat pocket and a garrote in my hat lining. A hydraulic mechanism pulled up the gate, and Gillespie motioned us forward. But I sat there like an eejit. For the life of me, I couldn't remember how to drive.

As I muttered a quick Hail Mary to calm myself, I felt the weight of the Judge's large hand grab my shoulder. "Steady, boy. Nothing to be afraid of. See the guards in the towers?"

I sucked in a deep breath. "Ain't we perfectly safe then?" Maybe he rightly feared a prisoner's attack, but what I didn't much like was the prison itself. I'd spent six months of 1921 in Belfast's Crumlin Road Gaol while the Irish armed struggle against the English staggered to a stalemate. There I cooled my heels, awaiting the king's pleasure for my own hanging.

I distracted myself with an old song, stuck in my head since I woke up that morning.

"This day we lay him in a cold clay bed,

Stones for his blanket, wet earth for his head.

This night do I hear him, key in the lock,

Lifting the door latch—Crow not, old gray cock."

"That's nice. Real nice." The Judge pulled a hip flask from his pocket. "I haven't heard 'The Gray Cock' since I was a little child."

"My gran, back in Carrickfergus, called it 'The Revenant's Regret.'"

"*My* ma always maintained the fella wasn't dead at all," he said, "just spirited away to abide under a faerie mound."

Mother Dolan had obviously cleaned the song up for the kiddies. "He sounds pretty dead to me. 'Forsake thy grave and shroud,' his lady tells him."

The Judge shrugged, took a swig of gin, and offered the flask to me. "Might as well fortify yourself with a 'wee drop o' the cratur.' This is apt to be a trying day."

I shook my head. I've never much had a taste for alcohol even though I grew up over a Belfast pub and had made my living for the past couple of months driving moonshine around the countryside for the Judge.

Earlier on that June morning, he'd offered me a step up in his organization, his usual driver being out sick. I jumped at the chance; I needed to do well at my first civilian job.

I'd spent my entire adult life murdering Ireland's enemies. It was high time to do right by myself and my family for a change. But the Judge hadn't mentioned the trip was to the Missouri State Penitentiary to witness a hanging at the convicted murderer's request. "Trying" didn't even begin to describe the situation.

I stepped on the petrol pedal, and the car lurched forward. Chains squealed and strained as the gate closed behind us. I steered through the portcullis—a sort of well-guarded entry tunnel—and into the prison yard, my heart pitter-pattering like a frightened rabbit's.

The first large building we encounter looked to be a dining hall. At least that was my assumption from the two lines of denim-clad prisoners marching into the place, the white men through the main door and the black prisoners through a side entrance. The noonday sun fried them all, white and black alike, as they shuffled along, heads bowed. Each extended his right arm to clasp the shoulder of the man in front of him. A guard waved me toward a parking spot behind the dining hall. The biggest cat I'd ever seen lounged in the space where he wanted me to leave the Model T.

I motioned the guard over to our idling car. "This here's Judge James Dolan. To see the warden."

"Yeah, yeah, mac. We know. The scaffold and seats for spectators are taking up the front parking lot today. Y'all need to leave your car here and walk through administration to the warden's house." He pointed out a building I can only describe as a castle among the maze of thick, high walls and massive structures surrounding us.

The clear feeling of threat—and not from prisoners or guards or heatstroke—about swallowed me right then and there. The penitentiary's stone walls radiated ill will as if hate had been quarried from the river bluffs along with the limestone blocks to build the fortress.

I started to argue with the guard, but the Judge chimed in, "It'll do me good to stretch my legs after the long ride. We mustn't upset the prison routine."

"Thank you, sir. We appreciate y'all cooperating. For everyone's safety, of course."

I sighed and crept the Model T toward the parking space the guard had pointed out. The cat made no effort to move. I tapped the horn, and he deemed to look up at the car, then lay his head back down.

"Goldarn Roscoe, you lazy, good-for-nothing—" The guard ran at the cat and brought back his foot to kick him, but the animal beat him to the punch, leaping into the air with a hiss and confronting the guard, hackles raised.

We needed no cat jinx to make our day any worse. I crossed myself as I climbed out of the car and took my time to scan the prison yard as I buttoned my suit jacket. "Sure ain't you got that animal's back up now?"

The guard spit. "He's a good mouser, I'll give him that. But about more trouble than he's worth, if you ask me."

Roscoe watched us from under some straggly shrubs. I tipped my hat to the offended animal. "Sure I be begging your pardon now." He sprang out of the bushes to run across the yard.

"You're coming with us, right?" I asked the guard as I opened the door for the Judge.

"Naw. Got orders to wait here for the sheriff. He gets to do the hanging." He mimed the drop, holding his head at a distressing angle and lolling out his tongue.

"How lovely for him," I said, "but do you think it's safe for the Judge to wander about with the inmates?"

"Don't mind them prisoners," he indicated the hundreds of men lined up for their meal. "We get visitors through here all the time. Just had the Jefferson City Garden Club come by last week."

The prison yard *was* a bit of a showplace. The hateful limestone-block buildings bound a large park complete with blooming flower beds and a couple of greenhouses. Might be mistaken for a university quad if you didn't look too close.

Best get the job over with, I thought, and helped the Judge out of the car. He'd sentenced dozens, probably more, of these men to this very prison. And each of them awaited the Judge's arrival with spoons sharpened. I'd no doubt about that at all.

I grasped the Judge's elbow and pushed him along at a smart clip. We faced quite a long walk to the administration building's shelter and shade. By the shortest route the castle still looked to be about the length of a hurling pitch away. I squared my body between him and the chow line. A paltry defense, and I knew it. The sun pounded my dark blue suit as we crunched in silence down the meandering gravel path through the flower beds and hedges. The Judge panted but didn't protest my pace as I eyed the prisoners for the first sign of attack. It helped my nerves, in a way, to worry over something specific.

Near the front portcullis, an old white prisoner with a farmer tan sheared the shrubberies along the castle's foundation. Unlike the other prisoners, he wore a white uniform. Roscoe, the giant cat I'd offended earlier, lay in the cool dust under the bushes, batting each beheaded branch as it fell. The old man stopped his chore and snatched his cap off his head in a respectful gesture, but from the look on his face he clearly hated the Judge.

Damn, I thought. We're made.

"Ain't it a fine day, sir?" I mumbled as we approached.

The old man gave me the once-over. Something about me seemed to confuse him, but I couldn't imagine what.

I hustled the Judge through a stone archway into the portcullis—out of the sun, at least—and we were directed to the warden's house.

He paused to catch his breath in the shade of the administration building's front portico. "That old trusty back there, he sure looks familiar."

"The hateful one with the garden shears? Ain't a lot of these men been in your court, now?"

"Not him. I'd remember. But I think. . ." he looked a little worried, "someplace else."

I could imagine no social circle that would include both the Judge and a prison trusty and was, frankly, pretty distracted by the din of banging hammers and the smell of fresh-cut timber. A squad of prisoners were constructing a scaffold off to our right, on what was normally the gravel car park. Beyond them, beyond the prison walls, beyond the corn fields, I could see the Missouri River, its banks green with trees and freedom.

"Never mind. Probably not important." The Judge pointed to a large Victorian home across the way, fronted by a clipped green lawn and a white picket fence. The warden's lodgings were within the prison walls but also a world away. "There. That's the house." He marched across the car park toward it, ready to be somewhere else, even if it was in the company of his not-friend, Warden Walther Stout.

A big, blond, sweaty guard on the porch, Thompson gun at the ready, blocked the stairs as he looked us up and down. "Hanging's not till four o'clock."

"Yeah, we know"—I eyed his name badge—"Nowak." All I wanted was to get my charge away from the prisoners and myself out of the sun. "Sure ain't we here to see the warden? This here's the Judge."

"Is he now?" Nowak spit on the yellow flowers drooping about the porch stairs. "Don't know as that the warden's expecting company."

Sweat trickled down my neck and back. "Your funeral, mac." I turned to leave. "Specially invited guest. State judge, on the prison and parole boards—"

"I remember now," said the Judge, wiping the sweat from his face with a handkerchief. "The trusty back there's been up for parole a couple of times. Boaz Jessop from Cadence County."

I shrugged. "I'm supposed to know that place?"

He glared. But I guess he didn't want to dress me down in front of the mouthy guard. "Hill country south of here. The board reviewed his case a few months ago."

"Guess he didn't get parole."

"No. He's benefiting from the structure here."

"Youse talking about old Jessop?" Nowak said. His voice dropped to a whisper. "He went crazy as a loon back in 1900 and chopped up his whole family."

1900. The year I was born. I tried to imagine spending the span of my lifetime in this place.

"He's saved, now," the guard said. "Done give his life to the Lord Jesus and got baptized."

The Judge frowned and swatted at a huge fly buzzing around his face. "Yes, yes. So he said."

A short, baby-faced guard with undercut hair burst out of the house and onto the porch, tightening his tie and putting on his hat. "That there city bastard here yet?"

Nowak spit at the flowers again. "Yeah, Willians, they's here. Just confirming identity." He waved us up onto the porch with his machine gun. "Can't be too careful."

Willians had the sense to at least look embarrassed about his "city bastard" crack.

Murmuring "Warden'll be with y'all in a bit," he led us indoors to stand in the foyer and then stalked off into the depths of the house.

And so, we waited. There stood Judge James Dolan, arguably the most powerful man in St. Louis, hat in hand on the doorstep of a outstate, politically appointed prison warden. The Judge tapped his foot as he examined the grandfather clock, the hat rack, a framed marriage certificate, and a gallery of stern family photos.

The longer we waited, the tighter the foyer felt. I could barely breathe the stuffy mothball-scented air and could hardly move without bumping elbows on the dark, spikey furniture or the Judge himself. We were caught like a couple of mice, trapped in a box.

Trying to act calm and in charge, I fought every instinct to shove the Judge out the door and hightail it back to the city. "You really think you owe this prisoner a visit then?"

The Judge looked away from a daguerreotype of some particularly homely Confederate soldiers and regarded me without his usual smile. "The case was hard, Sean. And the evidence a little *too* good. Peter Hervieux worked the barges his whole life and never got into any real trouble. Last year he jumped ship in one of those little burgs along the Missouri River. Told his friends he was getting too old for a roustabout's life. He wanted to be able to go to mass every day. I don't entirely buy that.

"Anyway, he got himself hired on as caretaker for a convent; every single one of those nuns was a character witness for him. However, he had no alibi, his hedge shears and work boots were bloody—"

"He was an outsider and a black man."

The Judge shrugged. "A couple of witnesses from the town testified they saw him fleeing the scene of the crime with the weapon. The prosecutor brought me a neat package tied up with a big red bow. I had my doubts, yet the jury—"

He talked on; I half listened, all the while pretending every single thing about the prison, from the guards' lip to the stone walls' hostility, wasn't troubling me.

Eventually the short guard, Willians, returned and ushered us onto a screened-in back porch. Through the wire mesh I could see a green lawn with cornfields in the distance, beyond the prison walls. A white-clad figure tended the warden's lawn. Boaz Jessop, the shrubbery trusty who hated the Judge. He dug weeds up by the roots with a thin, sharp blade. They did trust him indeed, it seemed. I didn't.

The sound of footsteps approached. A medium man in every way—height, weight, age—joined us on the porch, a cool customer in a pale blue seersucker suit. He had to be the warden, but my eyes just sort of slid over him. While invisibility is a quality I admired and cultivated, I had to wonder just how this fella commanded a prison full of hard men.

"Jim." With no change in his expression at all, he extended his hand to the Judge.

The Judge, however, greeted the warden with a firm handshake and slap on the back. "Walt, you old coot. How are you? It's been too long, too long."

I'd listened to a litany of Walther Stout's failings as a law enforcement official, a man, and a human being all the way from St. Louis to Jefferson City and was, once again, impressed with the Judge's acting skills.

"Let me introduce my driver, Sean Joye."

"Sure ain't it grand to be meeting you, sir?" I offered my right hand. "I've heard so much about your fine work here."

Warden Stout looked me over, head to toe, and obviously didn't like what he saw. He could probably spot a felon a block away. Eventually he accepted my extended hand to give me a moist, unenthusiastic handshake. "Black Irish, eh? Well, you'll have to do something about your accent. No Americans will be able to make out a word you say."

I'd found Americans expect all the Irish to have red hair, a flexible arrangement with the truth, and a weakness for the cratur. One out of three ain't bad, I guess.

I gave his hand an unnecessarily firm squeeze. Petty, I know. Another of my many flaws. He winced, and I crowded him a bit closer. Stout had an inch or two on me, not enough to matter. I caught and held his gaze and flatten my voice, "Fair point. I'll work on it."

He looked away and took a step back.

"Well, Walther, the kid's just off the boat," the Judge said. "He's doing fine, considering."

"In the city, perhaps." The warden had recovered his snide tone, but he kept his distance. "All foreigners there, anyways." He glanced at the short guard. "Show this man where to get some lunch, Guard Willians."

At that point, no longer interested in discussing my faults, the Judge and the warden started to catch up on the doings of the various political hacks of their mutual acquaintance. I thanked my lucky stars I didn't have to eat with them and followed Willians toward the kitchen.

He flung open the door and pushed past a pale woman in a sack of a denim dress, obviously a prisoner, struggling with a lunch-laden tray. I held the door as she sailed passed me toward the dining room. "Don't trouble yourself," she said, muttering under her breath, "ya lousy screw."

"Just a visitor, sis," I called after her. "I ain't looking for no guard job."

The kitchen stank of hot grease and sour milk and was even warmer than the rest of the house, despite a roaring exhaust fan that filled one of the windows. Williams cocked his head toward the departing woman. "Don't even bother with her. That there bull dy—"

Maybe he suddenly remembered he wasn't in the guards' mess hall. "Dago," he corrected himself, "won't give you the time of day."

"Italians' not giving me the time of day ain't a problem." I had to shout in his ear to make myself heard over the fan. "Hate to think you ask your female prisoners for 'the time of day.'"

He flushed. "Ain't you city folk got no sense of humor? Nothing like that happens around here. Against regulation."

I decided not to pick a fight with a guard on my first day in prison and offered my hand. "I'm Sean Joye."

"I'm Jake. Jake Willians," he said, giving my hand a squeeze. "From Ireland, eh?" He waved me toward an oak-plank table, two places set for lunch.

Despite the stench and the roar of the fan, the room tried to be homey. Red rooster-patterned curtains flapped in the fan's draft, and a black-and-white checkerboard design tiled the floor and walls. I shrugged out of my suit jacket and hung it on the back of a chair as Williams shouted at the cook, a gray-haired black man dressed in trusty whites, "Turn the goldarn fan off. Can't hear myself think."

He hurried to comply. We sat in silence; I guess Williams was trying to think of something to say. I drank an entire glass of cool, sweet tea in one gulp.

"You alright, youngster?" the cook said. "Kinda red in the face there. Don't be getting no heatstroke." He refilled my tea glass.

"I'm OK." I drained half the second glass. "Thanks."

He turned a small oscillating fan toward the table. A blessed, blessed breeze chilled me.

Williams at last blurted out, "Bet you is glad to be safe away from them there revolutionaries in Ireland. I seen a newsreel about that Michael Collins's funeral last year. Bad business."

Being as I'd been one of them there revolutionaries in Ireland not so long ago, I didn't express an opinion. Just then the door flew open, and the woman prisoner sauntered in, her tray tucked under her arm.

"Well, pigs are slopped," she said to the cook.

He started to laugh, glanced at Willians, and plastered a solemn look on his face. I hid my smile with more tea drinking.

"No call for lip, Miss Trina," the cook said. "Find yourself cracking wise in the blind cell."

She shrugged broad shoulders and wiped sweat from her face. Her features were strong and expression forthright, skin olive-toned but pasty, and dark hair bobbed. Not in a fashionable way, more like the barber had cut around a bowl on her head.

"Hey now," said Willians, glaring at the two prisoners. "You know better, Inmate Morland. Inmate Galliani ain't no 'miss' around here."

"Sorry, boss." Mr. Morland began to fill a couple of plates with potatoes, green beans, and fried chicken.

"I'll let you off with a warning. This time."

I watched the woman the cook had called "Trina." She touched the old man's arm. "Thanks. Don't get in no trouble on my account." She picked up one of the plates and a breadbasket and strode over to the table. "Comrade," she announced.

It took me a minute to realize she was talking to me.

"The Socialist Peoples around the world," she said, "Russia, Italy–even America—continue to support the Irish Struggle."

Trina slapped the basket on the table. "Soon the masses everywhere will rise up to shake off their chains. When that day comes, the Six Counties held hostage by Britain will be free."

"What's you yammering about now, Inmate Galliani?" Willians said.

I just sat there, slack-jawed. "Ah, thank you." I rose from my seat. "Won't be seeing a united Ireland in my lifetime, I expect." I turned to Willians. "She means the peace treaty in '21 with the English. Our leaders bargained away part of the island to end the War for Independence."

A little frown formed around Trina's mouth, and wariness crept into her eyes. "Ya ain't pro-treaty are ya?"

About the last thing I expected to discuss on a hot summer day in Middle-of-Nowhere, Missouri was the intricate details of Irish politics. I lifted my chin and leveled my gaze at her. "I stood with General Collins to the end. And after. In Free-State's colors." Well, not literally. Most of my squad didn't have actual uniforms, our intelligence work being top secret.

She spit in the plate of food as she handed it to me, muttering what I was pretty sure were Italian curses.

"Pro-treaty" was the wrong answer, I guess.

Willians jumped out of his chair and knocked her to the ground. "Galliani, damn you. Always gotta push it." As he raised his fist to hit her again, he shouted at the cook, "Get on that there telephone and call over to the women's unit for the matron."

"No harm done, now is there?" I said, clasping Willians's shoulder and pulling him back. "Often been tempted to spit in my *own* food of late."

"This ain't none of your beeswax." Willians shrugged my hand away. "She's always pulling some sort of bullshit." But he lowered his fist.

Trina leapt back to her feet, straightened her dress, and looked amused. "The Oppressor can chain my body, yet he will not silence the Voice of the People. I will speak the truth to power every day of my life."

Willians stared at her, hard and long. "I'll learn you a proper attitude, so help me God. You is going in the blind cell, Galliani," he spluttered. "Don't care if it *is* off the women's ward. Inmate Morland, put down the telephone. Fetch Guard Nowak in here."

The cook obeyed as Willians said to no one in particular, "Ain't no natural woman, no how."

"You really want all this bother on the day of the hanging?" I said. "A lot of extra work for no real harm done."

"How 'bout you don't tell me how to do my job, and I won't tell you how to do yours?" Willians's tone could've stripped varnish. "Cons'll run right over you if you let 'em." He looked over at the woman, who commenced whistling a revolutionary tune— "The Internationale," I think—while she scraped the food from my plate into a slop bucket. "Ain't that right, Inmate Galliani?"

"Matron will have something to say about ya going behind her back."

About then Porch-Guard Nowak slammed open the back door. Willians handed Trina over and returned to the table. The cook brought us our food, but the scene had left my stomach sour. The heat had taken my appetite, anyway.

Willians plastered a smile on his face, tucked a napkin into his collar, and picked up a fork. "We got us a treat here, today, Mr. Joye. Company food. Don't we, inmate?"

"Sure thing, boss. Warden likes to feed his guests right."

The guard had a coming appetite and shoveled in the meal as I buttered a roll. Out the window, high puffy clouds gathered in the distance, although the sun still baked the prison. I caught a glimpse of Guard Nowak dragging Trina through the front portcullis. My guts twisted in sympathy, but I reminded myself she wasn't nothing to me. Still, I went to the window for a better view.

The guard and Trina passed the burial detail I'd seen earlier in the day. The inmates marched along, shovels and pickaxes over their shoulders, free, at least, from their leg irons. Then the old trusty, Jessop, appeared out of nowhere. He gave Trina a good long stare as she vanished into the portcullis tunnel, and then he approached the burial squad.

As much as I wanted to keep my head down, powder dry, and get through the day with as little bother as possible, I had to stick my nose in where I had no business. "What's going on out there?" I asked the cook, busy at the sink with dishes.

"Hmm," he said. "Don't rightly know, sir."

Jessop gathered the tools from the inmates, who patted him on the back and shuffled away.

"Oh, I see," said Mr. Morland. "Inmate Jessop's gonna put their tools away, so they can get to lunch before the dining hall stops serving."

"Well, ain't he a prince."

"Hey, now, you two," Willians said as he sauntered over to the stove. "Shut your trap, Inmate Morland." The guard helped himself to seconds from the pots on the cooktop. "Mr. Joye, the cons ain't allowed to speak to guests. You'll land him in the blind cell."

"Sorry." I kept my eyes peeled for Jessop's next move. The old man, struggling with the shovels and pickaxes, made his way across the car park and plopped himself down on the warden's back porch steps, the dirty tools clattering against the cement. He pulled a red bandana out of his pocket and spread it out on the porch.

"Inmate Morland's right, though. Inmate Jessop's the helpful sort. He's got duties all over the prison, the farm, and the factories." Willians peeked over my shoulder out the window. "But he's got no call to clean tools on the warden's porch." He handed his filled plate to the cook. "Hold this a second whilst I run him off."

Jessop had commenced scraping dirt off the tools onto the bandana as Willian banged out the back door. "What's the matter with you, Inmate Jessop? Warden don't want no dirt all over his porch."

"Sorry, boss. Clean it right up, I will." Jessop stuffed the bandana in his pocket as he hoisted himself up. He balanced the tools on his shoulder and took off.

"We ain't got many trusties, nowadays," Mr. Morland told me as he put Willian's plate on the table, "and three done up and died last week."

"Flu?" I parked myself back in my chair, picked up a fork, and made furrows through the mashed potatoes on my plate.

He shrugged. "Didn't have no flu. Strong men, in the prime of life, just went to sleep and didn't wake up the next morning."

That was suspicious as hell. I guess no one particularly cared about convicted criminals up and dying all of a sudden. Well, maybe the other convicted criminals did.

Willians rejoined us and motioned the cook for more sweet tea as he settled down to the table.

"So Jessop's had to step lively," I said. "What with the trusty deaths."

Willians scowled like he was struggling to remember how much he'd told me about the old man. "Ah yeah." Willians chewed on a chicken leg while he thought about it. "He done took up the slack right well. Usually, he's a male nurse in the hospital."

"Guard Willians," the warden's voice floated through the kitchen door.

The guard dashed into the dining room, napkin still tucked under his chin and chicken leg in hand.

Mr. Morland refilled my sweet tea glass. "Inmate Jessop's a power doctor, so they say." He glanced over his shoulder and then whispered, "even though he killed his whole family."

I gave him a bit of side-eye. "A what-kind-of-doctor?"

He shrugged. "He cures the fever by the laying on of hands. Works the root, maybe."

Before I could ask the man what "work the root" meant, Willians returned.

"Warden'd forget his head if it weren't 'tached. He wanted to know what time's the hanging." He frowned. "Now this food is cold."

"Warm it in the oven, boss?"

"Naw. Chicken's just as good cold." Willians dug back into his meal. "What was I talking about?"

"Jessop's a nurse."

"Yeah, yeah. Thought we'd lose Inmate Hervieux to the flu last winter and save the state the expense of an execution. But Jessop, he pulled our star prisoner through. Spent every spare moment after his regular work was done at Hervieux's bedside, down there in the basement ward."

"They were particular friends?"

Willians looked at me like I was stupid. "You know Hervieux's a colored man, right?"

"I've heard that about him, yes." Jessop's charity toward a black inmate sounded unusual, in Little Dixie, anyway, as this part of Missouri was sometimes called.

The guard seemed determined to get a rise out of me. "Don't y'all stick with your own kind in the big city?"

I'd stuck with my own kind—Irish nationalists, most of them Roman Catholic— my entire life. Can't say as the practice had done me much good at all. Standing, I tossed my napkin on my plate, unable to sit at table with the man another minute. "Getting by in the city, I've found many other qualities in a person to matter much more."

Willians's gray eyes flashed, and he stood as well, napkin bib still dangling from his collar.

"Please, sir," Mr. Morland hustled over to the table with dessert, "you ain't gonna leave without trying my pie, now is you?"

Me and Willians stood down out of respect for the slab of blackberry pie Mr. Morland presented to each of us. Pie, I could eat. The next few minutes were quiet except for the chewing and contented sighs.

"Was Jessop just being kind to Hervieux?" I hazarded to ask, "with all the extra nursing?"

"Not sure." Willian's scratched his head. "I thought maybe Jessop was witnessing, you know, aiming to save Hervieux from the flames of Hell, there on his deathbed. He's a jailhouse preacher, he is."

"And Hervieux's part of his flock?"

"Hell no. He's about everything Old Jessop's not." He held up a greasy finger. "Colored." He raised a second finger. "Papist, not a Christian."

I opened my mouth to correct him but thought better of it. No point in arguing.

Willians ticked of a third finger. "River man, not a mountain man." He made a fist and smacked it hard against his open palm.

"All those two have in common is being murdering devils."

I lifted my eyes to the sky again and watched the clouds pile themselves up off to the south. Willians grunted through a second slice of pie. I was worrying over what they'd done to Trina on my behalf when the Judge called out to me from the dining room, "You coming, Joye? Time to hear whatever it is Hervieux has to say to me."

***

Me, the Judge, and the warden followed Willians through a maze of walkways, locked doors, and antechambers, stopping to be searched and questions a number of times. Well, the screws searched and questioned *me*, and the Judge let them. It was altogether too much like my time as a prisoner of war in Crumlin Road Gaol. A sour knot of tea and blackberry pie hurt my stomach.

Willians whistled a happy tune and wacked his billy club along the bars of death row as he made for a pool of light at the far end of the corridor. "Rise and shine, inmate. Got a visitor." He halted at a small cell.

Through the bars I could see a dark-complexioned fella of average height and wiry build sitting on a bunk. I'd expected more menace, somehow, after everything I'd heard about this man convicted of murdering the nun who'd befriended him. In fact, Peter Hervieux had a pleasant and open air about him. His face, half paralyzed and with a nasty scar running across his left eye and down his cheek, lit up at the sight of the Judge. Somehow the injury didn't mar his appearance any but rather set off the dimples in his right cheek.

"Hey there, Inmate Hervieux," Williams brandished his billy club as if the man could somehow escape his cage and attack us, "no false moves."

"Of course, Guard Williams. Sorry," Hervieux murmured and perched on the bunk's edge. While the Judge barked something bossy at Williams, a familiar, if muffled voice, hissed at me out of the darkness, "Hey, comrade. Over here."

No one else paid Trina any attention. I ignored her, too, eyes peeled for any threat to the Judge from Hervieux.

Every nerve in my body tingled with the danger I sensed all around us. I knew the source wasn't the man locked up in front of me. I kept on telling myself I felt threats from long ago and far away. And menace was part and parcel with the cellblock's peeling shards of green paint and the gapped-tooth grin of the iron bars. The whole place had me spooked.

The condemned man inclined his head to the Judge. "I greet my honored guest." His voice had the slow drawl of the deep South. Kinda peaceful. A relaxing voice.

"Peter Hervieux. So, you're about to meet your namesake," said the Judge. "You'd be better off talking to a priest than to me." He turned to Willians. "This is ridiculous. Open the cell."

Trina persisted to fuss at me out of the darkness. "I'm sorry for spitting in your food. If ya was with Michael Collins in the early days, then ya helped strike a great blow against the ruling class."

I trained my attention on Willians, who was protesting to the Judge, "Against regulations, sir."

The Judge threw the full weight of the state judicial system at the man; Willians didn't stand a chance. The door to the tiny cell squealed open. "Wait out here, Joye," the Judge said. "Not enough room in there to swing a cat."

Willians manacled the prisoner to his bunk and stood over him, truncheon at the ready. Did he really think Hervieux had a play here? More like, just tightening his grip because he could. Hervieux seemed to take it in stride though, a pretty minor indignity in the big scheme of things.

"Welcome," Hervieux said, offering the Judge a seat on the bunk opposite him as if it were a fine easy chair.

I watched from outside the cell and spoke over my shoulder, "No harm done, Miss Galliani. And yeah, I done my duty."

Hervieux was speaking to the Judge, "My friend, a priest is but a vehicle—his opinion doesn't matter. But *yours* does."

Trina continued to hiss at me, "Don't be such a stuffed shirt. I'm Catrina. Trina to my friends. Ya gotta name?"

"Sean."

"Please to meet ya, comrade. So does your boss there know?"

"Know what?" I still refused to look at whatever dark hole they'd flung her into. "About the war?" I'd told the Judge just enough, although he acted like he knew plenty more.

I'd enlisted in the cause when I found my way to Dublin and into Michael Collins's squad before I was even twenty. We worked directly for the general without much in the way of chain of command and few written orders. My war record was redacted for the most part.

"No. About you. Being a—queer?"

I spun around. "What?" Where did she get off saying something like that? I was a married man. Had been, anyway. And what could she know of me from talking together in the warden's kitchen for all of two minutes? About Irish politics, at that.

I looked back at the cell. Two men sat in a pool of light, the Judge and Hervieux deep in conversation, and Willians stood by, slowly slapping his cudgel against his palm.

I followed Trina's voice through the gloom to a thick iron door. It had a closed slot at eye level, perhaps large enough to pass through a bowl of porridge.

"Sorry," Trina whispered, "queer's not quite right." At least she'd piped down. "Some kinda jocker. Tough guy."

I jabbed open the slot and found myself glaring into total darkness. I slammed it shut.

"Now I got it. You fancy the sheiks *and* the shebas," she said. "Well, don't get no ideas about me. Ya ain't my type."

I took a deep breath and glanced at the death row cell. The Judge seemed to have forgotten I even existed.

Lighting a cigarette, I said, "Sure what do you be wanting of me?"

"A stick of chewing gum would be nice."

I fished half a pack of Beeman's out of my pocket and, opening the grub slot, passed it through. "Anything else?"

"It don't make me no never mind who ya fuck. Just wondering—"

"I'm sure nothing unnatural will ever happen again," I said. I wasn't at all sure, although I'd convinced my confessor, and more importantly myself, that any sins I'd committed while young, lonely, and drunk were in the distant past. "So, what's your story, sis?" I was puzzled as hell as to what her play might be.

"Oh, the usual proletariat struggle. The military-industrial complex fingered me as a threat—threw me in here with my sisters-in-arms. I'm the last of the lot from the days of the draft protests."

It's hard to remember, now that the Great War is long over, except for the parades and memorial building, but the whole enterprise was pretty unpopular in the States, particularly when the draft started. A lot of citizens—not just immigrants, anarchists, and communists—went to jail under the Sedition Act just for speaking their minds.

I heard her open a foil wrapper and the snap of her teeth biting the gum. "What else do you be wanting of me?" At least she was distracting me from odd fancies about dangers lurking in the prison's very mortar and brick.

For a moment, all I heard from the tiny window was chewing. "I need outta here, today, or I'll tell them about your 'unnatural' ways. Which ain't true, ya know. Love is love."

"Sure I'll be taking my spiritual advice from a blackmailing atheist now."

Trina laughed, "Just do it, comrade."

"You got some kinda appointment for the evening?"

"Maybe." She passed the gum packet and foil wrapper through the aperture. "Take this, so the matron don't find it in here. When you get me sprung."

I laughed, too, trying to sound nonchalant. "Don't hold your breath." Every instinct told me she was trouble, a wild card in a situation that could go wrong in so many different ways. Women bring a single-minded ruthlessness to revolution. At least, in my experience.

"Just tell the matron I'm here." Trina lost her sass. "The patriarchy bypassed her authority. She'll be pissed. Ya owe me that much, don't ya think?"

I moved back to Hervieux's cell without answering her and leaned my forehead on the cool bars, aiming to calm down and decide what to do about Trina.

The prisoner paused whatever he was saying and looked up at me. "Who have you brought with you, my dear Judge Dolan?"

Somewhere in the building a metal door clanked, and voices echoed.

"Just my driver," the Judge said.

"Hurry it up, inmate." Willians slapped his truncheon against his palm. "Say your piece. Your dinner's coming."

Sure enough, Jessop was trudging down the corridor, tray in hand. "Sean Joye," I told Peter Hervieux. "Sorry for your troubles."

"Mr. Joye. An honor." He shot me a knowing, lopsided grin and winked. Maybe he could tell I'd been inside, the smell of Crumlin Road gallows still clinging to me. These prisoners were all up in my business, it seemed.

Willians searched the dinner tray for contraband, and then waived the Judge out and the trusty in. While me and the Judge stood in the open doorway, Jessop arranged the tray for Peter and salted the blood-red beef steak bits, baked potato, and dish of red beans and rice.

"Alright, Hervieux, I've indulged you: I came all the way up here. We've rehashed your whole trial," said the Judge. "You got anything else to tell me? Like owning up to the murder?"

"Again I say I am innocent of this crime, my dear Judge Dolan. The real killer roams free. You must intervene with the governor."

"I don't have all that much influence," the Judge said.

A lie, and we all knew it.

The trusty produced a pepper shaker and showed it to the condemned man. Peter gave him a nod, and Jessop bent over the tray to season the food. As he straightened back up, he stumbled into me. I caught the old man and a full serving of pepper, and then some, right up the nose.

"So sorry, Mr. Joye," Jessop muttered as I sneezed into my handkerchief.

"Hey now, inmate," Willians cuffed Jessop's ear with the back of his hand. "You know better than to touch the visitors."

The Judge studied his shoes. "I'll have a mass said for you," he told Peter. "High mass with all the trimmings at the new cathedral in St. Louis. I promise."

Willians hustled us out and shoved Jessop down the hall. He raged all the while about the penalty points the trusty had just earned for assault of a visitor with pepper. I imagine Trina enjoyed the show.

** *

The Judge seemed distracted as we walked back to the warden's house. Mr. Morland served us sweet tea in a closed, stuffy parlor where we hunkered down for a few hours to wait for the execution, the Judge in an easy chair, me in a rocker.

We'd no more than sat down when the warden strode in. "Well, Jim, some of us have to work for a living. I'll be over at my office." He turned on his parlor radio. It hissed and crackled as it warmed up. "I believe there's a ball game you lollygaggers could listen to."

The Judge didn't even look at him. The warden turned to me. "Ball game?"

"Sure," I said, not caring a whit. I didn't know the Judge particularly well, but clearly Peter had got to him. Every so often he'd utter some legal mumbo jumbo, more to himself than me. At last he helped himself to the telephone.

And Trina had got to me. I didn't take her threat of a morals accusation, which could land me in jail if not straightaway deported, all that serious. Mostly I hated the thought of her sitting in the dark alone and helpless.

As I pictured Trina in the blind cell and listened to the Judge speak with various switchboard operators and state-government flunkies, demanding to talk to the governor, I shivered. Then sweat. My head swam then my stomach churned. I wanted the execution to be over. I wanted to go home. Of course, I felt like a heel, wishing another man dead so I could have a lie down in my own bed—well, borrowed bed—in my brother's little apartment above his bar back in St. Louis.

I must have fell asleep because, before I knew it, someone was shaking my shoulder. "Your boss wants you," Willians said. I struggled to my feet.

The Judge and warden stood in the foyer. "I'm going to stay near the telephone. Waiting for a call from the governor," the Judge told me. "Go out to the viewing area with the warden and keep an eye on things."

"What things?" I slipped on my suit coat. As I was in a shivering phase, its warmth felt good. "You're the thing I'm to keep an eye on, I believe."

"There's a guard on the porch. If the governor doesn't call me back by four, I'll be right along. Save me a seat."

"Time's a wasting," the warden said. The clock struck three in agreement as we followed Willians out of the house. We paused on the shady porch while Willians locked the door behind us. An old ragtime crowd-pleaser filled the air courtesy of the penitentiary's well-regarded inmate band, arranged in a makeshift bandstand near the scaffold.

I was too tired to go off on a wild goose chase for the women's matron like Trina wanted, but I did have the warden's ear, for a moment at least. "The Judge noticed a woman prisoner in the blind cell, back there in the men's area. Kinda irregular, it seemed."

"What?" The warden said. "Who?"

"The woman serving lunch at your house today. Inmate Galliani."

"My federal prisoner." Sweat sprung from his forehead.

"Seemed odd to the Judge." I put on my hat and ventured down the steps into the sunshine, wishing I had a straw skimmer like the warden. Much more suited to the hellish American weather than my felt fedora. At the foot of the stairs, I turned back to face the warden. "Word to the wise."

He whispered something to Willians, and the guard shot me a dirty look. "I can't imagine how that happened," the guard said. "I'll take care of it right away." He bounced down the steps and took off, double time, toward the prison complex proper.

The warden joined me and led the way toward the scaffold. "The Feds don't have a women's prison, so they send their females here. We're under a great deal of scrutiny," he wiped his brow and adjusted his skimmer, "especially in regard to the high-profile anarchists. Since Goldman and O'Hare wrote those books, the press—"

I nodded and concentrated on not vomiting on his shrubberies, while he pushed on toward the gravel car park. "What exactly did Trina, Inmate Galliani, I mean, do to land herself here?"

He halted his march to the scaffold, but at least we were under a shade tree. The warden glanced around. We were alone. "She's quite famous. The press bestowed the moniker 'Dynamite Doll,' which stuck in the popular imagination. You'd know her by that name, I suppose."

Well, Trina sounded much more exciting than she let on, but I had to shake my head. "I've only been in the States a few months."

The warden shrugged. "We've had her custody since 1919. She planted a bomb in the Stock Exchange Building in Chicago. A policeman was killed, and several more officers were seriously injured." He recommenced his stroll toward the gallows, and I followed.

"Galliani aiming for an 'Attentat,' eh?"

The warden slapped the back of his neck, crushing a mosquito. "The anarchists *claim* to be peaceful."

I smiled, thinking on a few anarchists I'd known in Ireland. They'd pass through the cause now and again but most didn't find a congenial political home with us. "The corrupt, oppressive system will die under its own weight," I said, mimicking their standard lecture.

"So they say." The warden clearly didn't share my amusement at anarchists' attitudes. "Then some godless foreigner attacks the very foundation of democracy with a big, splashy, act of violence. All for publicity. Well, I'll show her some 'Attention.'"

Although I didn't object to government, per se, like the anarchists did, as a physical-force republican I'd no room to criticize Catrina Galliani. The warden stewed in silence on the pending bad publicity, I guess, as we headed to the gallows.

By the time we arrived, most of wooden folding chairs arranged at the foot of the scaffold were occupied by spectators, and a crowd milled around behind them. A thick blue haze of tobacco smoke hung over the congregation. At the sight of the warden, the band launched into "Stars and Stripes Forever." We might as well have been at a political rally. Maybe we were.

The warden waved at the crowd and pointed me toward the front row. We sat, and I concentrated very hard on a spot on the ground. Band music blared around me, while time ticked away.

The sun pummeled the white gravel, heat bouncing up only to be caught in the blanket of smoke and pushed back down onto the crowd. Perhaps it was my fever's fancy, but the smoke hovered over the scaffold and fed off the crowd's nervous energy. It became a being I could practically touch, a being made of pain and hate.

It was hard not to watch the hands of the clock on the prison façade creep around the dial. About quarter to four a guard appeared at the warden's elbow. They whispered back and forth, intense sharp hissing, while everyone in the place stared. At last the warden got up and followed the guard.

"Goldarn governor," said a lanky farmer type a few chairs down from me. "If that animal gets a reprieve—"

"Hush, hush," a tired-looking woman next to him said, "you don't know for sure."

We all sat and waited some more. The heat, smoke, and brass band did nothing for my spinning head. The Judge joined me a bit after four PM. He stared at his hands in his lap. The muttering and shuffling from the back of the audience grew louder and more uneasy. Another fifteen minutes ticked by. The musicians, having apparently played everything they knew, started over with "The Entertainer" again.

"Joye," the Judge gave me the eye, "go see what's going on."

"Leaving you alone here don't seem like a good idea."

"Pshaw. There's lots of guards around." He patted his left chest. "And I've got a little protection myself."

Grand. He brought a gun to prison. Guards had patted me down all day long but hadn't the nerve to touch His Honor. Knowing he was armed didn't make me feel any better at all. Nevertheless, I could see this wasn't an argument I'd win, so off I went toward the prison proper. Behind me, I could hear horns quacking off randomly as the band quit in mid measure.

"Please remain calm." The Judge took charge of the situation. "I'm Judge James Dolan of the Twenty-Second Circuit Court. I've just sent my assistant to inquire—"

I swam through the hot, damp air of the front portcullis tunnel, retracing my route from earlier in the day to emerged into the deserted prison yard. Apparently, the whole penitentiary was on lockdown for the hanging. The flowerbeds wilted in the late afternoon sun.

I cut through the black prisoners' cell block like we'd done earlier in the day. Rhythmic clanking and snatches of conversation followed me as I made my way down corridors and through checkpoints, headed to the isolation building. "Dead on his bunk," I heard out of the darkness. "Just like the others."

Peter's tiny cell was full of people: the warden, a couple of guards, a doctor, a priest. They huddled around the prisoner's bunk. At the sound of my footsteps, the warden looked up. "Hervieux's dead."

The room spun and went black.

***

Thinking back on that day, I have to wonder why I wasn't more disturbed to find myself wandering a wasteland, blinded by the light of the red sun. The land was parched, dusty swirls rising to follow me as I shuffled down a hard, packed dirt road. Not a bit of green on the landscape or bit of blue in the sky. I walked a long way without seeing a house or farm, let alone another person, although in the far distance huge, slab-like structures, unlike any buildings I'd ever seen, towered on the horizon.

This place sure wasn't Missouri. I had a sinking feeling it was Purgatory. Contrary to rumor, they are not the same place.

My soul was restless, driven to push on, despite my body feeling done with it all. The sun never moved, just beat on me from directly overhead. On and on I put one foot in front of the other, until I fell, exhausted, to the ground. Perhaps I slept awhile, if the dead can sleep.

A twangy voice woke me, "John. Johnny Joye," and I found myself in darkness. Darker than night or a black bag over your head. Maybe even darker than the blind cell. And why was this joker calling me "John," the English version of my Irish name? I guess Americans run Purgatory, like everything else.

I realized I was out of the sun and the air was cooler, at least. Although I was pretty sure one of the circles of Hell is made of ice. The darkness was getting on my nerves. The simple solution would be to open my fecking eyes, but, try as I might, I couldn't do it. I'd fallen flat on my face in Purgatory's wasteland, but I was definitely lying on my back, my arms crossed over my chest. I willed my hands to reach out, but they refused to budge.

I don't mind saying, as weary as I was of Purgatory, finding myself back in my lifeless body wasn't any improvement. Panic rose, and

I made to call out. Except I couldn't. My mouth wouldn't open. My throat wouldn't move.

I lied to myself that I'd seen worse trouble. Either I was dead, a revenant trying to rise, or more—maybe less— optimistically, I'd been buried alive. Some of my senses weren't working so good at the moment, but I tried for a calm and orderly recon of the situation.

I could definitely smell things—fresh cut pine, dirt, and hay. A dead mouse. I sure smelled my own scared-senseless sweat.

And I could feel pressure—I wasn't exactly lying on a feather bed. No, the spot was hard but with a bit of give to it. Not metal. The air was damp. Cool, wet, and close. Stale.

Terror fueled a surge of strength, and I managed to lift one hand off my chest. It bumped into a hard, rough surface. Wood. When I made to pound on it, my hand barely moved. Again and again I tried to shout out but made not a sound.

Just to latch onto a rational thought, I reviewed my army training. Mock execution to shake up prisoners was a tried-and-true British practice in the king's attempts to control the Irish. I just needed to tell myself it was mock and that whoever'd done this would come back soon enough to torture me in some other way.

I abided like that for a good while, in and out of consciousness, not entirely sure if I dwelt in stages of dreaming or under a fairie mound. Most likely, dead and gone.

Still, I felt compelled to escape the grave, driven by my unfinished revenant business or simply the need to survive. I aimed to thrash and kick and scream, a river of fury coursing through my veins. But I couldn't move, and the rage about burst through my skin.

I resolved to keep a good thought; to act alive is to be alive, right? Of course, that's probably what all the revenants tell themselves.

Just then, I heard sounds. Real sounds, not my imagination. Muffled and far away, the beautiful sounds of gunfire and rough voices shouting. Blessed, blessed dogs barking. I couldn't *actually* be buried, very deep anyway.

With mighty effort I could kick a leg and throw a punch. The box—I was, indeed, in a box—rocked maybe an inch. I kept at it and taught my limbs to move again, wiggling then jiggling as best I could. But the box wouldn't budge. It was as if a great weight held it down. I tried not to picture the mound of earth piled upon my coffin, so, naturally, the image loomed all the more clearly.

Making one last, all-out try, I kicked hard enough to rattle the box. With a second burst of energy, I managed to tip it on its longways edge. I teetered on the brink for a moment, then crashed to the floor where the box broke into pieces. I was so happy not to be buried, the pain of my ten stones' deadweight falling a couple of feet bothered me not at all.

I'd landed flat on my face, was still practically paralyzed, and may have broken something important in the fall, but I managed another roll to the left. I clenched my teeth and strained every muscle in my face to open my eyes. Flickering light filtered through chinks where the roof joists met the thick stone walls of the building. I could make out large, rectangular pine boxes stacked among slabs of ice packed in straw. I was in the icehouse, I concluded.

I lay in the dirty ice and concentrated on regaining command of my limbs, still wondering if I was to be a revenant now, like in the old songs, my dead body roaming the earth to settle some pressing business. Yet I couldn't think of anyone who'd excessively mourn my passing and need my comfort. I'd neither hidden a fortune nor particularly desired revenge.

I managed a roll to the right, aiming to locate a door, but instead found myself face-to-face with the body of dear departed Peter Hervieux. He was surrounded by pine shards, much like I was. His box must've been stacked atop of mine. His eyes snapped open, and he moaned, "Yesss.

Coming." His eyes were clouded over, and he sure wasn't talking to me.

He rose to his feet, stumbling toward the door. "Coming. I'm coming."

Somewhere in the back of my mind, I heard a whisper, "Arise and come to me." As suddenly as I'd heard the voice, it was gone. Perhaps all this bother was part of my Purgatory; now I was being called to my reward.

After a couple of swipes at the table edge, I grabbed it and pulled myself to my feet. I sort of tossed my hand at Peter's shoulder and managed to stop him. "Mr. Hervieux."

He turned, fists clenched. But the mistiness in his eyes had cleared a bit, and they begged for help.

"You hearing someone, too?" I asked.

"Must go," he held his head like it hurt, "to Jessop. He has witched me."

Had I heard Jessop? The nasal twang didn't fit any angel or demon I could imagine. "Just a second there." With great effort I moved so as to block his way to the door. "How—"

"Coming," Peter said, eyes again glazed over. "Let me by."

"Just a minute, sir. Tell me—"

"Must . . . go . . ." Peter threw a punch, but I dodged. Truth be told, I lost my balance, falling down just as he swung his arm. I flailed about on the ground, stuck as if in thick honey. Actually, the both of us moved in slow motion.

I struggled to my feet. "We gotta fight Jessop, not each other."

Peter landed a glancing uppercut to my jaw, while his left jabbed me in the breadbasket. His eyes brightened, and he looked more like his usual self. "Ah," he said. "You are wrong, my friend. This activity distracts us from him."

"Grand." I avoided his next blow but then fell over a great pile of ice blocks and landed on my keister. "Got any idea what he's up to?"

Peter threw himself on me. "If the Judge wouldn't call—governor." We wrestled about, clumsy and slow, in the straw and mud for a bit. "Jessop," he continued, "would work the root." He paused then panted, "Hide me away," as he hooked his arm around my head, "in death."

I whacked at his ear with a chunk of ice. "How's that an escape plan?"

"He'd bring me back." Peter's hand squeezed my wrist. "So I could slip away." As I dropped my melting cudgel, he said, "Or escape in a coffin."

"Then someone would dig you up?" The plan was about as daft a one as I'd ever heard, and I didn't know what he meant by "work the root."

Before Peter could clarify, Jessop piped up in my brain, "Listen to the voice of the Lord, speaking through me." With strength

I didn't know I had, I pulled away from Peter's grip, twisted, and pinned him to the ground. "Not bloody well likely," I said aloud to Jessop.

Peter reached up and grabbed me around the throat. He was the stronger man, and my limbs still didn't seem to be working very well. "Don't pay him no mind." Peter sounded faint and far away, like sheep bleating on a hillside. "Listen to me. Follow back to *my* voice."

I struggled to focus on the man throttling me. To hear his words. To take in their sense. My grip on him loosened.

Peter seized the moment to deliver a wicked left-right-uppercut combination that landed me flat of my back and seeing stars. But he knocked Jessop clean out of my head. For the moment, at least.

Revenants or not, we needed to make ourselves scarce, away from whatever Jessop had in mind for us. "Jessop's escape plan was a piece of shite."

Peter helped me to my feet. "Agreed, my friend." But since we'd stopped fighting, his speech grew slow and eyes dull. "I expected to die as he worked the trick on me." His face slackened, and he stood stone still, hunched over. "Better than hanging." His lips twisted as he struggled to speak, "Never did I think he'd make me—zombie." He shuffled toward the door. "Must go—to him."

I'd never heard of a "zombie," either. Some sort of revenant servant, I guessed. "You ain't gonna be no zombie for him. Maybe we can distract each other enough to keep Jessop out of our heads while we get away." We pushed open the icehouse door, Jessop's annoying voice just a drone in my head, lecturing me on my sins and imminent doom. But I already knew all that.

The night air was still and almost as hot as midday though it was well past sunset. Heavy clouds hid the moon and stars, and smoke drifted and curled around us.

"Which way?" About then I noticed neither of us wore a shoe or sock on our left foot. "What the feck does this mean?" Maybe the prison people rushed through preparing our bodies for burial, but my money was on more of Jessop's "working-the-root" shite.

Peter didn't answer either question. I figured he was listening to Jessop's call. And while I could hear the old man myself—"Come to me. Open the way for the day of the Lord's Judgment"—he seemed to be making a bigger impression on Peter, who stood stock still, his eyes again cloudy.

I managed to will my arm to slap at Peter's face, although I couldn't put much force behind it. "Snap out of it. Don't listen to him."

He blinked and came back to me. "Oh, right." I pulled him into a nearby building's shadow, and he leaned in close so I could hear him over the din. "When I was sick, Jessop visited me many times to lay on hands." Peter smelled about as gamey as I felt. We *were* dead, after all. "Then he'd ask me to tell the old bayou women's tales of the bokar— a witch—who could call men from their graves to do his bidding." He looked a little embarrassed. "Stories to frighten children, but I guess I enjoyed impressing him."

We crouched in the dirt along the foundation, while I peeped around the corner. I could hear the men inside the cellblock, rattling bars, pounding walls, and shouting themselves hoarse. It seemed odd for the guards to let such behavior stand.

"I never heard no stories about witches calling folks from the grave. In Ireland, the revenants in the old songs pretty much have their own agenda of unfinished business." Of course, the other side of the veil was a big place. I make no claim to understand much of it at all. I knew the fae to be lying, conniving, thieving bastards. Still, we call them the "good people," so as not to offend and make matters between our folks any worse.

"I never heard of no free zombies." Peter smiled his crooked smile. "I'd like to learn such a song. In exchange for a beer, perhaps."

"My singing is only middling fair . . ." I went slack, my mind flying off far away as Jessop whispered at me again.

Peter's voice called me back, "How goes it with you, my friend?"

"Old Jessop's loud and bossy. And I can hardly move."

"Sing to me now," he said.

I just stared at him, unable to understand what he meant.

"Your song?" Peter said. "Of the free zombies? Music might distract as well as fisticuffs."

"Ah." I struggled to think of the words to "The Revenant's Regret" and force out the tune. "Ye do . . . walk the earth . . . and sleep in it, too?" Singing was hard, but at least Jessop's words were drowned out by my own. "From Faerie ye steal—" As my singing grew louder, I couldn't hear Jessop at all. "Such a trick we will rue."

He whistled the tune, quite a feat with his scarred lips and cheek. "Like that?"

"Yeah, you got it." Jessop was gone, at least for the moment. "The song goes on to tell of the revenant visiting his wife at night, then he must return to the grave before the rooster crows at dawn."

"He calls me to the scaffold," Peter struggled to his feet and then helped me stand, "so we should go the opposite way, toward the back gate."

It crossed my mind the Judge could've got himself in some real trouble while I was dead. I hadn't imagined those battle sounds;

a ruckus of some sort was going on up ahead. "Let's check out that commotion first." We crept through the shadows toward the glare of electric lights and the racket of angry shouts, breaking glass, and occasional gunfire. I was sweating bullets, and it wasn't all from the heat.

A battalion of guards stood at attention, floodlights and Thompson guns trained on the dining hall. They took no notice of us, intent they were on the limestone building, fairly shaking on its foundations. A prison official called through a megaphone for the dining hall inmates' surrender. With the hubbub so loud, I doubted anyone heard him.

A revolution must've taken place while we were dead. And I really needed to find out what had become of the Judge. As we watched the standoff, several prisoners appeared at the hall's front door, a couple of guards strong-armed before them as shields.

"Stay back," an inmate called out. "Preacher says it's high time for the reckoning."

"Hold your fire, men," a guard shouted.

The prisoners took the opportunity to stream out of all the doors, throwing rocks, hunks of wood—anything, really—at the lights. Many broke, immersing the yard in darkness except for the cheery fire visible through the dining hall windows. "Judgment time," someone yelled. "Fuck, yeah," another answered. "Lord's coming to deliver us."

"My car is right over there," I shouted in Peter's ear. "We can drive through the flower bed then out the front portcullis. The Judge is most likely in the warden's house." I hoped.

Peter struck out toward the car parked behind the dining hall. He seemed to have pretty well gotten used to being dead. At least he moved faster than me. I struggled just to walk.

One look at the convicts all over the yard—running, fighting, scaling the walls—and it was pretty obvious whoever organized this party had only invited the white prisoners. I imagined the black inmates had the good sense not to be out and about in this free-for-all. And while I could've been killed again through the exuberance of the rioting prisoners or panic of the guards, Peter was bound for trouble.

We wove through guards and prisoners locked in hand-to-hand combat, beating at each other with pavers, meal trays, and soup ladles. Peter got to the car well ahead of me, cranked the Model T to life, and flung himself behind the wheel.

I stumbled onto the passenger-side running board. "Wait up a fecking second." I could tell Jessop was talking to Peter again as he looked up, struggling to keep his cloudy gaze fixed on me. He pointed at the back gate, just a few hundred yards away. "Please understand—"

I did understand. He owed me nothing, and his best chance at life was to escape now, in the confusion.

As Peter gave the car some petrol and jumped on the gear pedal whipping it into reverse, sweat trickled down his mangled cheek. "No, no. I will not come to you." With obvious effort he pushed the pedal to change gears, and the car leapt forward, aimed for the back-gate portcullis.

"The world is ripe for Judgment," Jessop said in my head. "I call you to this place of separation, holy unto God, that you may purify yourself and be clean, ready for the great day. It's too late for your boss but maybe not for you."

I tried to ignore him by shouting at Peter, "*You* gotta understand—" maybe protecting the Judge was my revenant job, "Jessop's got the Judge." I pounded the side of the car, "Turn around!"

Peter ignored me, swerving to avoid prisoners running about every which way as he navigated the short stretch of driveway to the back gate. The escape route he'd picked depended on friendly inmates, or at least chaos, having charge of the back portcullis. But Peter's luck ran out. As he pulled into the tunnel, shouts of "Stop that car" greeted us. A half dozen men mobbed the Model T and pulled me and Peter to the gravel road.

My sluggish limbs found some energy right quick, and I twisted, turned, and ducked away from the cons. Peter made a break for it, and I followed, running back toward the prison yard.

"That's right. Come on over to here," Jessop's voice encouraged me, like he knew somehow the tight spot I was in.

But just as we slipped passed the crowd at the portcullis, another group of prisoners grabbed us. They dragged me and Peter right back to the source of the riot. In the shifting firelight off the dining hall, I could see the guards abandoning their posts and falling back toward the administration building. They'd be of no help at all finding the Judge, assuming I could even get to them.

The prisoners roughed us up a bit as their ringleader, the big, freckled redhead from the burial detail, looked me over. "Fuck. Not a guard. I saw him drive in this noon. Might make a good hostage though." He motioned for his men to leave off punching me. "You someone important?"

"I'm a barrister," I said. They looked puzzled—yet respectful, I thought. Maybe I was in the clear for the moment, but Peter was crouched low to the ground, protecting his head and midsection from a rain of blows and kicks. "He means he's my *lawyer*," he managed to shout over the inmates' curses. "Here for my burglary appeal."

"Naw," the big ginger insisted, "You is that fucking nun-killer." He pointed to me. "Lock him up for later."

A couple of inmates started to hustle me away. One said, "I heard that motherfucking Hervieux was dead like all the others," as he dragged me away.

His mate, who'd latched onto my other arm, observed, "Knew it was fake."

I could hear Peter protesting, "Not me. I'm an innocent man."

"Yes," I shouted over my shoulder as I struggled to free myself, "You got the wrong fella."

"Bullshit," was the last thing I heard as the prisoners threw me into a nearby outbuilding. I fell into what felt like a great pile of crockery and banged my head against something sharp. Pain jolted my skull, then settled in for a slow burning ache behind my left ear.

Dirty glass walls and rows and rows of flowerpots surrounded me. Getting out of this place wouldn't be hard, even if the door was locked; it was a greenhouse for Christ's sake.

But did I want to get out, that was the question. Firelight danced in the yard, flickering through the grimy glass and silhouetting the riot. This greenhouse wasn't a bad place to sit out a bad situation. Just how far did my obligations to a convicted murderer, charming as he might be, and a less-than-honest judge go?

Jessop's voice was in my head again but merely an annoying buzz in the distance. Whether he'd been knocked out of my mind by the inmates pummeling me, or I'd found the strength to ignore him, I didn't know, but I felt much more in control of myself. I was pretty sure it was my conscience, not Jessop's promptings, that whispered concerns about the man like as not already killed by his fellow prisoners. Maybe I was still walking the earth to protect Peter.

"Sure Peter Hervieux's been sentenced to death for a heinous murder by a court now, ain't he?" I argued with myself. Though the American legal system dispensed no more justice than the British one. My few months in America had already taught me its black citizens had few rights and even less protection under the law—Jim Crow law, some called it. And outside the law? Even more dangers.

The prison cat pounced out of nowhere, cutting a small squeak short. He padded over to me, delicately winding his way among the broken pot shards and uprooted seedlings to drop a mouse by my face.

"Thanks, Roscoe," I said. "Not really needing a snack at the moment."

He sat down by the mouse and stared at me.

"I know, I know." I made a vain attempt to brush the dirt off my suit. "Since when do I care about a court's opinion?"

He scratched his neck and bit at his fur.

"What about the Judge? Yeah, yeah, I took on the job. He made me, you know? Work for him or do the time." When I first came to America, I'd fallen in with—let's just say, "the wrong elements" and got nicked doing something stupid. By sheer luck—good or bad, I hadn't yet decided—I ended up in the Judge's court. "I'd no choice in the matter at all. And there was no mention of anything like this."

The cat cocked his head to one side.

"What would General Collins say, you wonder?" I reached out to scratch his head, and he perked up, nuzzling my hand with his face.

"Well, Roscoe, he'd say don't ask so many fecking questions: Complete the mission. Leave no man behind. But he's dead now, ain't he? Should've followed his own advice—gadding about the countryside in an open car, seeing the sights. What was the man thinking?"

Something else still gnawed at me—that Trina woman's jeers about betraying the revolution. What did she know of my life? "I did my duty," I explained to Roscoe. "Why should I take on other men's troubles?"

He looked skeptical but pushed the mouse toward me.

"Naw. You have it." I stroked him again. "You're a good man." I felt cloth under his long, thick coat. He was rigged out with a sort of pocketed vest. "Why, you little smuggler, you." I looted his cargo—a few cigarettes, a pack of Doublemint, a Baby Ruth bar, and several notes. Roscoe munched his mouse, in no way concerned I'd just stolen all his parcels.

I ate the candy while I read. Mostly on raggedy pieces of paper or gum wrappers, the notes were what you might expect among prisoners: "I owe U 5 cents." "Afta chow. LyburE." In the dim light the pathetic little messages blurred and swam before my eyes. "Comrade J: R Causes unite. U choose hour corrupt Courts fall."

Sure didn't that sound bad for the Judge? "Bloody hell." I extracted a final note from Roscoe's vest. "I suppose I should gather up the energy to go find him." Reckoning from the thin but sturdy paper, the note had been cut out of a Bible. It scolded, "The congregation shall rescue the manslayer from the hand of the avenger of blood. The congregation shall restore him to his city of refuge to which he had fled."

"Jesus-Mary-and-Joseph." I crossed myself and swallowed over the hard lump in my throat. The message was clear enough; Peter was the one I needed to save.

I shoved the contraband in my pocket, and in doing so discovered I'd been carrying around a red flannel bag. I sure as hell hadn't ever seen it before. It reeked like a bus station men's room and was full of dried leaves and dirt. Out of nowhere Jessop's voice boomed,

"Arise and seek this Judgment Day
And to thy Master's will give way.
I call thee now; he will greet thee soon.
Defy me not or meet thy doom."

"No!" I crumpled to the ground, my head on fire, my heart pounding, and my limbs flailing in their haste to obey.

Roscoe dashed away, and I flung the bag after him, into the darkness. And as suddenly as Jessop had started yelling at me, he stopped.

I sucked in a deep breath and then another. Wait a minute, I thought, I *feel* my breathing. Not only that, I *feel* my heart pounding. I bloody well *feel* my aching head. The mental fog lifted, just a bit. I took another deliberate breath, just to prove to myself I could do it.

Jessop had poisoned me at some point during the day, gimping me, body and mind. And the evil of this prison itself, along with what every prison, everywhere, will always mean to me, had gimped my spirit.

But I wasn't dead; neither a revenant nor a soul languishing in Purgatory. I was a living man with a pressing job to do.

I racked my brain for a rescue plan, as I made a trial of standing, then walking. I'd promised to help Peter, as God and Roscoe had just reminded me. And the Judge was— well, the Judge. Maybe I'd made a contract with the devil, but he was the devil I knew.

***

Yet I was still slow, unsteady, and not sure what good I'd be to anyone. The greenhouse door being locked, in the interest of time I wrapped my hand in my coat to break a hole through the glass wall.

The prison yard was lit only by fires and full of smoke, angry shouts, and a smattering of gunfire. Clouds thickened in the southwest, sending a stiff wind to whip the blazes higher and higher, showering sparks on nearby buildings. Thunder rumbled in the distance.

Although inmates had the run of the prison yard, guards in the towers continued to snipe at them with rifles. Even with the poor lighting, every now and again they managed to shoot a prisoner down.

The dining hall was engulfed by fire, and the nearby unit that housed black prisoners shook with men calling out for rescue. A squad of prisoners wrangled a fire hose toward the blaze. I prayed the guards would leave off shooting at them for a bit.

"Hurry up," someone called from the portcullis. "Y'all gonna miss the hanging." The inmate wasn't talking to me in particular, just announcing to the knots of prisoners in the yard that something interesting was about to happen out front. I had a horrible feeling that interesting something was meant for Peter.

I hoped to drive myself to the scaffold but found the car ditched at a jaunty angle in a flower bed, all four tires flat and the windscreen shattered. So I made for the scaffold on foot, passing the women's housing unit on my way. I wondered what Willians and the warden had eventually done with Trina. I hoped she was someplace safe, like maybe locked in her own cell. The woman was annoying as hell, but I kinda liked the cut of her jib. I melted into the throng pressing through the portcullis toward the front car park, no one paying me much mind.

Ahead of us, the tunnel exit framed a nightmare sky right out of a Judgment Day painting: Lightning crackled across the horizon. Massive clouds rolled in above the prison. Smoke hung in the air.

Guards hunkering down behind a barricade of automobiles blocked access to the front gatehouse. When a few men emerged from the portcullis, blinking in the glare of car headlamps, a storm of bullets mowed them down.

Prisoners returned fire with captured weapons, their shouts bouncing off the portcullis tunnel. "You'll git yours, copper," echoed round and round, "in the lake of fire." But cries of pain cut off the taunts.

The firing from the guards' barricade ceased, and I heard Willians's megaphone-amplified voice. "Attention, inmates. Y'all return to your cells if y'all expect to live through the night. The state police control the facility. There ain't no chance of escape."

At the far end of the car park, the scaffold still awaited a customer. A welcoming circle of what could only be candles winked and twinkled from the platform. A lone figure marched across the gallows floor, shouting at a small but growing audience. "Set your house in order, for God's Son is coming. Bend your knees in prayer to repent."

Jessop sure had command of the high ground.

He was awfully convincing, and his voice pinned me to the spot. As I reflected on my many sins, a prisoner called out, "Ain't but three or four screws out there." I was pushed forward by prisoners rushing the guards' barricade, a berserker fury upon them. Bits of brick smashed the car headlamps and the prison façade porchlights even as the screws fired into the crowd.

I lost my balance and fell, only to spot Willians wrestling with a prisoner, just about to get his head smashed against the stone curb. A megaphone and lies about the state police weren't much of a defense, after all. I'm not sure why I even cared, but I managed to fling myself on Willians's man. I think I surprised the prisoner more than hurt him, but he hopped up and took off.

Through the whole fight, Jessop's sermon rang out, "Yet we trust in the Lord's promise. From the fire will rise life anew. A new Heaven and a new earth. Be baptized in the fire and the Holy Ghost."

As I struggled to my feet, I pondered my best play: Take advantage of the confusion to murder Jessop. Wait at the scaffold for Peter's captors. Look for the Judge in the warden's house.

Just then I noticed a knot of men in prison dungarees, backlit by the lightning flashes, headed toward the scaffold. They'd strong-armed at least one person who stumbled along with a gunnysack over his head.

"We've got to get to the gallows, see?" I shouted in Willians's ear. "The convicts are about to hang someone." The inmates arrived at the gallows steps, and they had *two* prisoners, men in suits, in tow. They pulled the sacks off of their heads.

"Right," Willians said. "Hell, them there inmates got the warden and that city judge."

"Come forward, brothers," Jessop said to the men, then shouted to his congregation, "Open wide all the gates, sayeth the Lord your God." The crowd of prisoners tossed a murmur of agreement from man to man, back to the captured barricade, where an obedient squad launched themselves at the front gate.

The inmates marched the Judge and warden up the scaffold steps, positioned them over the gallows's trapdoor, and slipped nooses around their necks. They stood by, ready for Jessop's next command. The crowd of prisoners at Jessop's scaffold-altar bowed their heads in prayer.

Things were going south, damn quick.

Dark, thick clouds swirled overhead, and a cool gust stirred the air. Dust eddies twisted around the crowd, and soon the wind was howling among the buildings. Jessop's shrill tones rose above the din. "Lord, we have blazed the way. The graves shall open, and them that sleep shall rise." His voice fried every nerve in my body. "The firstfruits of the Lord's Resurrection await." Jessop looked at the sky, holding his arms aloft. "Lord," his words echoed around the courtyard, "come now. Come in judgment.

This corrupt man, James Dolan, awaits your verdict."

Time ticked away, and the Lord didn't appear. Jessop's throng of believers left off praying and started grumbling.

"Sweet Jesus," Jessop finally said. "You are always in our midst where any two or three are gathered in prayer. We'll just commence to testify, knowing you'll be along presently to judge."

This change of plan seemed to please the crowd, men calling out "tell it, preacher" and "amen," as well as "string 'em up" and "fuck the courts."

The warden looked shook. The Judge, red-faced, talked to Jessop, but I couldn't hear him. I wondered how he was playing it.

A few raindrops fell on us as thunder rang out. "Silence, prisoner," Jessop shouted at the Judge. He turned back to face his congregation. "Hear ye, hear ye. This court of the Lord God is now in session. James Dolan, you stand accused of corrupting your sworn oath to God to faithfully discharge your office, of forsaking your duty, of worshipping false, papist idols—"

"He's sore because he didn't get parole," the Judge called out to the crowd. "How many of you—much more deserving men—wait for parole? Why should Jessop go to the head of the line?" There was a bit of muttering from the crowd, but I think every last rioter knew he was well beyond the help of a parole board.

Me and Willians continued to elbow our way through the throng, making for the scaffold. A few men took a poke or two at Willians, but most were much more interested in what Jessop was going to do to the Judge.

"Alright, Jessop," the Judge said as calm as if he were sitting on his bench. "You made your point. Let's negotiate—"

"Silence, devil," Jessop snapped at him.

"I'm just saying if any harm comes to me or the warden here, your goose is cooked."

As I started to make a break for the gallows steps, a new voice rang out, "Here's another one for the noose, preacher." A few yards ahead of me, at the foot of the stairs, a knot of inmates held a bloodied Peter Hervieux. His eyes were clear and flashed with anger and a bit of panic. I hoped he'd shook the old man's influence.

"The long drop ain't for Brother Peter today," Jessop smiled. "At last y'all bring me the Key to open the way."

The prisoners looked confused, and their grip on Peter slackened. I thought maybe he'd be able to make a break for it.

"Brother Peter is the Key. Don't y'all know your Scripture?" Jessop said. "Bring him on up to here."

The inmates shoved Peter up the steps and onto the scaffold where Jessop's henchmen grabbed and restrained the struggling man.

"As our Lord Jesus gave the *Apostle* Peter the Keys to the Kingdom of Heaven, so will he give them to *you*, Peter Hervieux, all part of his divine plan."

Pushing inmates aside, me and Willians rushed the scaffold stairs. When the Judge saw me, relief spread across his face. I didn't know what he was so happy about; I was most likely about to get myself hanged alongside him.

But the Judge seemed to trust me to have a play and did his part, which was to distract Jessop. "I understand from the warden here you're a model prisoner. I'm sure the next parole hearing—"

"Get thee behind me, Satan," Jessop thundered.

Willians swaggered forward, almost upsetting the circle of flickering candles Jessop had arranged on the gallows's platform. "Inmate, this here's gonna hurt you way more than it'll hurt me."

But Jessop's gaze held mine. Electric shocks of pain pulsed through my skull. Trembling, I sank to my knees. Jessop, loud and insistent, echoed about in my head. His preaching voice faltered as he mentally demanded my surrender. I looked to Peter for help, but he was still twisting and turning to get free from the two inmates who held him tight. My eyes focused, entranced, on the flame of a large red candle, tied by shoelaces to two black candles.

As Willians lifted his hand to hit the old man, one of Jessop's followers grabbed and snapped the guard's arm. Willians screamed but threw himself on the man, the two of them tumbling off the scaffold platform.

Although I saw all these things, I'd no strength to react. Jessop had finally got the better of me. He beckoned me to come to him, and I obeyed. He presented me with a bulky gunnysack, and somehow I knew what to do, just like I was serving mass again.

Jessop looked up at the sky, the lightning sparking white, green, and purple waves of color deep in the clouds. "Lord, bless this work to thy greater glory." Sweat dripped off his face.

Peter left off struggling, and his eyes clouded over. Which wasn't good, but rather than help him, I felt it more important to fetch out a dirt-filled bandana from the sack. I poured lines of the dirt—the graveyard dust I'd watched Jessop scrape off the chain gang's tools—across the scaffold platform as the old man prayed, "In the name of the Father, Son, and Holy

Ghost." Peter, shoulders sagging, stood at Jessop's side.

"Put them there dimes in the center," Jessop told me, then shouted into the wind gusts, "I offer y'all payment for the graveyard dirt. Come git it."

The sack also held a mason jar filled with dust. I poured it out, making a line from the red candle to the scaffold steps as he shouted, "Follow this path to me. Retrace the trail your bodies traveled to the graveyard."

"Joye," the Judge shouted, though I only heard him as a distracting, distant whine. "What're you doing? Get me out of here."

Another thing Jessop had inside his circle of candles was a trashcan lid heaped with smoldering garbage. The charred remains of my shoe was in there, along with a work boot like the inmates wore. As I lit up the herbs, dirt dauber nest, and other junk Jessop had given me in the sack, at least I had the strength and presence of mind to fished out me and Peter's footwear.

Jessop didn't notice, busy reading aloud a bit of St. Matthew's gospel, "I will give unto thee the keys to the kingdom of Heaven: Whatsoever thou shalt bind on earth shall be bound in Heaven. Whatsoever thou shalt loose on earth shall be loosed in Heaven."

Peter shambled over to Jessop, who gave him a large key and the Scripture page. Peter kissed the verse, wrapped it around the key, and threw it in the fire.

Jessop seemed to be able to use his connection into my mind to know what I was thinking and doing. It was a neat trick, but I concentrated on *not* paying any mind to my own actions and managed to slip Peter his half-burnt shoe, hoping it would help him break free of the old man.

"Come here, Johnny," Jessop said to me, "Read from your book of Revelations." Try as I might to resist, I couldn't help but stumble over to him. He gave me a page of Scripture.

I stood there, eyes shut tight and mouth clamped close. But he pulled the words out of me, tearing up my throat in the process. "Behold, I stand at the door and knock." I didn't even need to read the words; he knew them and spoke them through me. "If any man hears my voice and opens the door, I will come in to him and will sup with him, and he with me."

"That's good, Johnny. Very good. Now finish the work."

The last item I had from his sack of junk was a glass doorknob. I knew what he wanted me to do, I'd figured out why, and it just wasn't happening. He couldn't make me. So I thought.

As I fought his command, fought the pain, Jessop sighed. "It ain't like fetching a bit of your Personal Concerns, with or without your say so, is difficult." He nodded to Peter who punched me in the nose, which promptly started dripping blood on the Scripture page.

Jessop grabbed the doorknob out of my hands, wrapped it in the bloody paper, and threw them in the fire. "Ye that sleep in the Lord, come forth! I call you in the name of the Lord your God to break the bonds of death, rise to your feet, and come to me. You will listen only to the still, small voice of the Lord, speaking through me. You will obey the Lord's commands, which I shall deliver unto you. Come to me. Stand before the Lord your maker, for Judgment Day is nigh."

His voice dropped to a whisper. The rest of his prayer was between him and God. "Lord, please, take me to my little children. To my dear wife. Ain't I atoned long enough?"

But to speak aloud, Jessop had to loosen the grip in my head. I gathered my will while he scanned the sky. "Why do you tarry, Lord?"

Unsteady, I raised my hand to slug him. "Because he ain't listening, ya bloody old sod." But before I could strike, he pushed me down and strode toward his audience, crouching low over the edge of the scaffold. His tone pitched sweet and tender, he crooned, "Let every soul yield itself to the higher powers."

I crawled toward Jessop and glanced at Peter, hoping for some help. But, no, his cloudy eyes still stared straight ahead, not taking in any of the hubbub around us.

A new sound, a rhythmic pounding from deep in the prison complex, began and grew louder and louder. Jessop had to scream to be heard. "For our Lord God holds all power; any powers that be, they flow from God's will. Whosoever resists the power, resist the Lord. Them who resist are doomed to eternal damnation."

"Amen," the crowd called out. "Testify, preacher. Tell it."

The pounding sound stopped, only to be replaced by shouts of alarm that echoed through the portcullis and spilled out onto the car park. Inmates rushed out of the prison. They tripped and fell all over each other, then scrambled to their feet to take off running again. The ranks around the scaffold grew quickly, and Jessop revved up his sermon, "Now, I say, now is the hour of the Lord!"

Still on my knees, I was poised to push Jessop off the scaffold when I noticed a few dirty, emaciated men in tattered prison uniforms, hands bloodied, creeping through the portcullis. The swirls of fleeing prisoners around them made way—no, ran away. Shrieking in terror like little girls.

But a much more immediate threat soon wrested away my attention. Barefoot, hospital-gown clad men stumbled out of the infirmary's front entrance. All wore confused expressions but wandered toward the scaffold, toe tags dragging through the car park gravel.

Jessop's message rang out over the screams and thunder, "Come, brothers. The Lord's harvest has commenced." He addressed the roiling clouds above us, "See, Lord? They come—back from the dead, they come, in their haste to meet you. To stand before your judgment as you separate your lambs from the goats. Uplift the righteous and cast down the sinners," he pointed at the Judge, "into the pit of fire."

I didn't know much about magic then, but I knew evil when I saw it. I grabbed Jessop by the pant leg. "What deal did you make on the other side of the veil?"

He shook me off and continued to talk to God, "You have granted me paltry powers, Lord, compared to your own. Yet I have followed your commands as best I can, and now is thy hour; be it in Heaven as it is on Earth. Bring us your Rapture, Resurrection, and Judgment this day. Your servants are ready." He raised his arms high.

Some inmates mobbed the scaffold-pulpit, falling on their knees and gibbering for Jessop to save them. But most held true to form and attacked what they didn't understand, hitting the revenant shamblers with boards, bricks, and fists. For the moment, at least, that worked pretty well—the dead went down and stayed down. 'Twas a great relief to their poor souls, most likely.

Through all the commotion Peter just stood there, eyes glazed and cloudy, clutching his burnt-up work boot.

I struggled to my feet. "Your pockets—" I said to him, "look in your pockets for a red bag."

He blinked.

I turned out his britches pockets myself without any luck but finally found the hex bag tucked in his waistband. I threw it into the fire. "Snap outta it and run, goddammit." I grabbed his shoulders and shook him hard. "You ain't getting no better chance."

He surveyed the scene from Hell unfolding all around us. I couldn't tell if he was still in Jessop's thrall or just amazed.

"I gotta get the Judge outta here," I said. "You're on your own."

At last Peter roused himself out of his stupor, his eyes suddenly clear, but rather than run, he made to grab Jessop around the neck. While the two of them struggled, I ran across the scaffold to the Judge.

"Git away from the prisoner, Johnny," Jessop shouted.

I found I could ignore him again, but my fingers fumbled to loosen the noose's slip knot. Suddenly, a shove out of nowhere sent me flying off the scaffold. It wasn't far to the ground, and several praying prisoners at the scaffold-turned-altar-rail broke my fall. I rolled to my feet and ran back toward the scaffold steps.

But Jessop, in breaking off his mind control to wrestle with Peter and then push me down, had lost whatever grip he had on the revenants. They seemed to be getting their bearings, more interested in the sights, sounds, and pure male-sweat-fueled raging energy of the scene than answering Jessop's altar call. Any man beating down a revenant soon found another two or three like creatures grabbing and pulling at him. They were clumsy, sure, but strong enough to do some damage.

The sky opened up to pelt us with chunks of ice the size of snookers balls as a new wave of the dirty, raggedy revenants pushed through the portcullis. But cemetery dirt in their hair wasn't the worst of their problems; I could smell their putrid stench from across the car park.

The revenants' skin was as tattered and decayed as their clothes, both hanging in strips from exposed bone. For some, entrails dragged across the ground. For others, sharp broken bones stuck out at odd angles, and a finger or toe joint lost its grip, dropping to the ground as they slipped across the ice-covered car park toward us. The revenants' jaws seemed to work pretty well, and their teeth snapped like they aimed to bite something. They attacked anyone within reach, though the few guards in the throng seemed to get extra attention.

While I gawked like an eejit at the menace approaching from the rear, a big revenant in a hospital gown plowed right into me, nearly knocking me over. I jumped back, only to run straight into another dead man making for the scaffold. He was answering Jessop's call, I guess, but readily grabbed at me.

The skin of his face had shrunk—pulled back to reveal a few bad teeth wobbling in black gums. His white glazed eyes were sunk deep in the sockets, and a black mat of hair hung limp. Long, dirty, broken fingernails and hands covered in fresh cuts and gashes pulled me closer—I didn't like to think how'd he got those injuries. A forearm bone poked through the striped prison uniform he wore—a style not used since before the Great War.

I'd no idea how to fight a dead man, obviously magic-ed in some way. But he didn't give me much time to think on that. His bony hands, strength coming from—I'd no idea where—kept pulling me toward his jaws.

I jerked back to throw him off balance, but he was planted firm. So I relaxed and rolled into his chest, knocking him over. Of course, he landed on top of me, not really a better situation. His snapping jaws clicked and popped inches from my ear.

Certainly, I ought to be able to take him down; he fought like a little child. I heard low moans as more black-and-white-stripe-clad revenants crawled toward us. I twisted away, but he was on me again, and neither a hard kick in the groin nor a head butt in the jaw had any effect.

Though he couldn't feel pain, he'd no strategy at all, other than biting. I wriggled out of his arms again, scuttled away, and found a short length of pine board as I got to my feet. Three snapping revenants now menaced, but not having the sense to flank me, they stood in a row, each trying to climb over his mate's shoulders.

Holding the board like an American baseball bat, I planted my front foot. "Bite this, buddy." I swung for all I was worth at my man's jaw. It broke at one hinge and hung loose and flapping by the other. He didn't even seem to notice. A second blow to the chest sent him sprawling back into the other two revenants, the three of them a twisted pile of snapping, snarling, and moaning enchantments.

I finally crawled back up on the scaffold to find Peter still hadn't run off. He slouched with his hands on the trapdoor lever, eyes cloudy and face a mask. At least the hail had stopped. Jessop smiled at the havoc. "It's happening," he said to me. "The Resurrection."

I grabbed his collar. "Fix this."

"I can't. I can't." He danced away. "The Lord's own harvest has begun. My root work affected just a few, a very few—the newly dead. All these others . . ." He spread his arms wide. "A miracle of the Lord."

I still had my cudgel and the suspicion that if Jessop was dead, all this foolishness would stop. The grip he'd had on me was loose. Understandable; the man juggled a lot of balls in the air at once. I went to swing the pine board at him, but he was a beat ahead of me. He motioned to Peter, who looked at me without a glint of recognition or of his real self shining through. He knocked the board out of my hands before I knew what was what.

"Peter, wake up." I slapped him hard. "It's Sean Joye. You gotta fight this bastard." Our eyes met, and confusion flashed over his face as he sank back into his blank, clouded expression. Desperate, I began to sing the old revenant ballad I'd taught him, "Ah, the cock's crow doeth scold him, last tryst is done."

His eyes brightened a bit, and I thought—hoped, anyway—that Peter recognized me. He looked back at Jessop.

"Get him, brother. String him up," Jessop said. "Just another papist already dammed to Hell. Send him on his way."

Peter quivered, fighting his own skeleton to stand pat. "Run," he gasped.

But I was rooted, too, Jessop's claws dug into my brain. In fact, he urged me to march myself to the noose. I stumbled a step or two, fighting it.

Peter glared at Jessop. "No. This I will not do." He clenched his teeth, his face a picture of agony, and I could well imagine the torments Jessop inflicted.

Now Jessop was the one sweating it. He'd used himself up to call all those revenants from their graves, force his will into me and Peter, and preach up a storm. That sort of thing takes a toll on a man. He looked tired. And Peter, with more strength of character than anything Jessop tossed at him, could now defy the old man.

Jessop seemed to be having some problems keeping me sorted as well. His connection to me ebbed and flowed. In fact, if I just set my mind to ignoring the pain he used to goad me on, I could follow the line back to him and see *his* thoughts. I saw the decision when he made it; to go all in on the last throw of the dice.

Jessop let go of me completely. His poison might still weigh me down and cloud my thoughts, but he was gone from my head.

"Peter Hervieux, obey the voice of our Lord as he speaks through me," Jessop thundered.

Pain roiled across Peter's face as he sank to his knees. He covered his ears, blood dripping from his nose and eyes. "Mercy, my friend, have mercy."

Now that I could think something like straight again, what I thought about was the Judge's gun. I dashed across the scaffold and caught the Judge by the lapels while Jessop nattered away at Peter. "The Lord's mercy shall be yours." He pointed at me. "Git him. Be the Lord's instrument for the greater glory."

"About time, Joye," the Judge sputtered. "What've you been playing at?"

"Your gun," I felt under his suit coat, "still have it?" I grabbed what turned out to be a .45 caliber Colt, just as I felt Peter's hands squeezing my throat. Lights flashed, and my vision dimmed and blurred. I managed to slip the pistol in my pocket rather than drop it as Peter dragged me away from the Judge.

He let go of me moments before I passed out. With his cloudy eyes shimmering white and bloody tears streaming down his face, Peter obviously wasn't at home. Jessop must've thrown every ounce of will he had into subduing the man, but he'd done it. Peter bound my hands behind my back, easily restraining me with a new, unnatural strength. He wrapped a noose around my neck.

"That's good," Jessop said. "You'll meet your namesake soon enough and can report this fine work for the Lord."

Peter didn't react to the praise, but the bleeding from his eyes stopped. He tightened the noose and then stepped back.

"Now come pray with me, brother." Jessop started shouting at the sky again, "Lord Jesus, we's ready for your coming."

"I—I—I—" The warden spit out the first sounds I'd heard from him all evening. "I heard the Lord's call. Long ago. I'm a born-again Christian," he whined, "just like you, Jessop. I was always good to you as a fellow Christian."

Jessop paid him no more attention than a gnat, his hands gripping the trapdoor lever. "Lord, shall this corrupt judge die first, at the end of the noose he is so quick to use on others? Is that thy holy will?"

As he prayed, the revenants, both Jessop's victims and the decayed gate-crashers, climbed onto the scaffold using any toehold they could find. Jessop's attention was caught up in tattling on the Judge to God. Peter's eyes cleared, and he seemed to notice things again, like the revenants making for us. He hurried to loosened the bonds on my hands.

"We gotta get outta here." I freed myself from the noose.

"Agreed. Most assuredly." Peter kicked at a revenant who'd just climbed up a support and onto the platform.

The wind was quickly growing to gale-force strength. It whipped round the car park, and more clouds, bright with lightning, piled up directly overhead. The thunder was nearly a constant roar. The convicts had mostly fallen back into the prison buildings to take refuge from the twister that seemed to be upon us.

The cyclone might've carried the Judge and the warden off but for the fact they still had nooses tight around their necks. Jessop clung to the trapdoor lever, staring at the sky, a rapturous look on his face. "Lord, Lord, I'm ready. Take me now."

"Jessop, stand down," I called out as I thumbed off the pistol's safety and took a firing stance.

"Give us a sign you want these sinners to be spared for the moment," he prayed, not even reacting to my words.

I gave him a sign, alright. But just as I fired, he ran to the edge of the scaffold, dodging the bullet.

"Welcome, sister," shouted Jessop at Trina who barreled toward us from the warden's house. "Do you have a message from our Lord?"

"I've a message from the People." She tossed a firebomb at the scaffold.

"Shite." In the split second between impact and explosion, I turned my back to the bomb, shielding the Judge.

The bottle of kerosene cracked with a whoosh, and fire exploded across the scaffold. I dropped the Judge's Colt in my haste to fish my knife out of my pocket and saw through the rope. While shoving the Judge off the back of the scaffold, I could hear Jessop blessing the whole disaster, "Jesus, this is the moment of glory. Take me now. All is completed as you ordained."

I jumped down after the Judge. Out of the corner of my eye I could see Trina fighting a headwind to run toward the front gates. Around us, the decaying revenants paid the fire no mind at all and continued to climb the scaffold toward Jessop. Some of their raggedy clothes caught fire, but they marched on, into the flames.

The fresher revenants—inmates Jessop poisoned and magic-ed, like me and Peter—jumped back from the fire and ran about in sluggish circles, at least aiming to get away. All the prisoners who hadn't already took shelter ran like hell toward any building not already on fire.

I dragged the Judge toward a cop car parked near the front gate, part of the deserted barricade. Around us the wind knocked men down, pulled signs off the walls, and made off with large bits of lumber.

"Walther's still up there," the Judge said, "and that Jessop man."

I pointed at the burning scaffold. "Do you think either of them has a chance?"

The Judge was a mess, rope dangling from his neck, soot and dirt all over his face, and clothes ripped. "I'm an officer of the court, Sean. I can't just run off and leave the warden to die."

"Get in the car and stay put." I handed him my knife. "Defend yourself if you have to."

He squared his shoulders and nodded. His eyes were cold. And it wasn't a circuit-judge sort of cold. The man had grown up penniless—homeless even, at times. I'd bet money he'd been in a knife fight or two.

The wind shoved me back toward the scaffold. Fire had engulfed most of the front portion. I crawled under the platform to find the trapdoor dangling open. I expected to see the warden dangling as well, but he wasn't.

I held my breath and climbed up through the trapdoor into the smoke and flame, only to fall to my knees from the heat. I couldn't see a thing for the thick smoke, pink from the reflected flames. The wind whipped up even stronger, and the smoke parted for a second, long enough for me to spot Peter. He struggled to keep some slack on the warden's rope while at the same time loosening the knot.

A roar, as if a train were bearing down on us, filled the air and rattled the scaffold. I gulped a few breaths of fresh air and ran to Peter and the warden. We clung together and held onto the warden as the cyclone passed.

I was glad to see Peter's eyes, although bloodshot from the smoke, were their normal brown color, not cloudy white. He made short work of the knot and helped me drag the unconscious man toward the trapdoor. He bestowed on me the briefest and brightest of smiles before dropping through the hole to the ground and disappearing into the hubbub.

The wind calmed down, and the smoke was suddenly as thick as ever. A coughing fit took me as I glanced around for Jessop but saw not a sign of him. I could well have missed him; the smoke was thick, and the flames fierce.

But I guess he was long gone by then. Or maybe the Lord really did rapture him. Then the loudest boom I'd ever heard exploded somewhere very nearby, and I pushed my man and myself through the trapdoor to the ground.

***

I drove the cop car out the open front gate just before a half dozen armored cars with mounted gun turrets rumbled through, pushing aside the useless barricade. A squad of state troopers piled out of a couple of trucks and quickly fanned out to secure the perimeter.

We'd traveled only a few hundred feet when I spotted a herd of reporters gathered around someone standing atop the prison wall, giving a speech.

It was Trina, of course. I stopped the car. "How'd the press get here so quick?"

"That woman called all the big St. Louis and Kansas City dailies from the warden's house," the Judge said. "Now, get me out of here."

Right about then, a squad of troopers surrounded her, Thompson guns at the ready. A dozen flashbulbs sparked the night as they hustled her away. Trina was mouthing off the entire time, but I couldn't make out what she said. The press, however, seemed to be lapping up every word.

"Drive, if you know what's good for you," the Judge said. As if on cue, thunder roared overhead, lightning cracked the sky opened, and rain poured down on us.

"Alright, alright." I hit the petrol and gear pedals and lit out into the dark. A few troopers shouted at us to stop, but they had their hands full, soon giving up the chase. Rain was pouring on Jefferson City, but we quickly drove out of it when we reached the main road back to St. Louis.

***

I got the Judge home around dawn. I begged off his wife's offers of first aid, fresh clothes, and coffee. I just wanted to be home but couldn't resist picking up one of his morning newspapers off the front lawn and checking the headline. "Deadly Prison Riot," a couple of inches high, splashed across the page. The sidebar was an interview with Caterina Galliani.

"The Dynamite Doll, a notorious Italian immigrant anarchist, claims responsibility for the prison uprising. Galliani stated to this reporter, 'Comrades, this glorious day is the start of the American People's Revolution. Power bubbles up from the masses and will be buried no longer. The oppression of the Worker, which has long reigned in this hellhole called Missouri State Penitentiary, has ended as the People shake off their chains.' She confirms the riot was planned, organized, and started by anarchists. 'I am one hundred percent responsible for this Attentut to inspire the Uprising of the People.'"

***

A week later, I was back at the prison to collect the Judge's car. Guard Willians, his right arm in a sling, met me in the car park and greeted me like an old army buddy. I guess we were.

It was another scorcher of a day. I'd invested in a straw boater, at least. "Everything back to normal?"

Willians pointed across the car park to where inmates were cleaning up the charred remains of the scaffold. "We gotta feed the inmates outdoors, what with the mess-hall fire. Whole place's still on lockdown, 'cept for work and meals." He walked me toward the Judge's Model T, parked in the shade of the water tower.

"Find all your escapees yet?"

Willians spit on the ground and looked disgusted. "All but the ringleaders, Hervieux and Jessop."

I'd read fifty escaped prisoners were recaptured, but Peter and Jessop were still at large. They remain so to this day. Although reports of Peter sightings in various burgs down the Mississippi floated across the Judge's desk from time to time, no one seemed to have seen Jessop. The general opinion was he'd disappeared into the Ozark Mountains.

"I last saw them on the burning scaffold." I lit a smoke as we strolled and offered Willians one.

"Don't mind if I do." After a few puffs he said, "Didn't recover no bodies from the scaffold fire."

"Newspapers say Trina Galliani was the boss, anyway."

He resumed our walk toward the car. "A woman? Not likely."

In addition to losing any chance of parole from her original sentence, in the fall of 1923 Trina was convicted of arson in connection with her firebomb at the gallows. She was sentenced to twenty more years of hard time.

I gestured at the warden's house as we passed it. "Warden Stout came through it alright?" Before my own escape, I'd left him, unconscious but breathing, on his front porch.

Willians looked somber. "His body's fine—a mite too much smoke to the lungs. Nothing broken." He shook his head. "He ain't himself. Jumping at shadows. Got a whole detail of guards to follow him around. And he don't go anywhere near the prison."

We'd arrived at the car and walked around to inspect it. "Mechanic got new tires on there. Y'all have to get the glass fixed in town," Willians said.

"Looks good. The Judge appreciates it."

He looked back at the clock on the prison facade. "Two guards were killed—good men, with wives and families. Friends of mine."

"Sorry for your troubles."

He smiled and lifted his bent wing. "Sixteen of us injured. That's all. Not too bad, considering."

I dropped the cigarette butt in the dust and ground it out under my foot. "I saw prisoners down." Twenty prisoners were shot, and five died of their wounds.

Willians shrugged. "They're lucky there weren't no more." He bit his lip and glanced up at the water tower looming over us.

"Out with it," I said.

"It's just—this place is getting to be a nuthouse. Not sure the job's worth it, anymore."

"Go on."

He whispered, "What happened to you, Mr. Joye? I saw you dead as a doornail. I put you in a coffin myself." His voice grew louder and his eyes blazed. "And Hervieux and the other dead inmates—men boxed up in the icehouse ready for burial? And what about the bodies in the hospital basement? They tried to escape through the parking lot." Our eyes locked. He was shook, barely hanging on. "We found them all afterwards, alive again."

"Well," I said, "I guess someone jumped the gun on calling us dead."

Willians spit on the ground. "We need us a better doctor."

I thought on the poor prison medic, sure to get sacked. But it was the only story people would buy. "Something else on your mind?"

"Well, the tornado hit the graveyard. Ripped out a big, old tree, like pulling weeds. Churned up a whole mess of coffins.

Bodies must've already done rotted away. But them goldarn inmates dreamed up a wild tale of the dead rising from up outta the ground. They's sticking to it, to a man."

We'd both seen the revenants rise that night. He knew it, and I knew it. He looked to me for a logical explanation, and I hadn't one to give him.

"Best put it out of your mind. Perhaps find a new job."

I wished I could do the same.

About The Author

Kathy lives and writes in St. Louis, Missouri, USA. Her novelette, *Water of Life*, was published in 2019. Her short fiction has most recently appeared in the Bards and Sages Anthology *Great Tome of Forgotten Relics and Artifacts (The Great Tomes Series, Volume One)*, with earlier works in *Bards and Sages Quarterly*, *Golden Visions Magazine*, and *Mused Literary Journal*. *Hippocrene* has published several poems. Follow her on Instagram at kathylbrownwrites and Twitter at KL_Brown. Kathy's blog, *Kathy L. Brown Writes: The Storytelling Blog*, lives at kathylbrown.com.

About The Typeface

This book's typeface is Century, originally designed in 1894 by Linn Boyd Benton of American Type Founders for *Century Magazine.* Particularly well suited to body text, the crisp and elegant Century family of typefaces have remained popular for periodicals and books for over one hundred years.

Follow Sean Joye's further adventures in *Water of Life*

A shell click-clacked into a shotgun's chamber. I knew that sound well enough and dove for cover behind a pile of lichen-covered boulders. My panted breath hung in the November air. And ain't that what comes from soft living? Riding around in automobiles all day took a man's strength as sure as sitting in prison for six months.

"Git on outta here." The old woman's voice was coarse. "It's mine now."

Although I could hear her, I could hardly see her through the dense wooded hillside above me. What I did see, most particularly and quite well, was the shotgun hefted to her shoulder and pointed square at the rocky outcrop that shielded me. For the moment.

It stood to reason she couldn't actually hit me. Caleb had described his grandmother as at least eighty, and I was a good fifty yards away. Nevertheless, I felt her bead right on me and that she had no qualms about dropping me where I cowered. Just another missing city slicker.